LOVE STORY

Oliver Barrett the Fourth is a big Harvard sportsman. He's rich, he's clever, he's good with girls. Jennifer Cavilleri is a music student. She's beautiful, she's clever . . . and she thinks big Harvard sportsmen are stupid.

When they meet, they fall in love. But is any love story without problems? Oliver's father is a rich banker in Boston, and Jenny's father is a poor baker in Rhode Island.

This is a story about different kinds of loving. Oliver finds it easy to love Jenny, but he can't learn to love his father. Jenny teaches Oliver about loving, about dying, about being strong. And Oliver learns that 'Love means you never have to say you're sorry'.

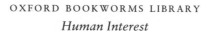

OXFORD BOOKWORMS LIBRARY
Human Interest

Love Story

Stage 3 (1000 headwords)

Series Editor: Jennifer Bassett
Founder Editor: Tricia Hedge
Activities Editors: Jennifer Bassett and Alison Baxter

ERICH SEGAL

Love Story

Retold by
Rosemary Border

OXFORD UNIVERSITY PRESS

Oxford University Press,
Great Clarendon Street, Oxford OX2 6DP

Oxford   New York

Auckland   Bangkok   Buenos Aires   Cape Town   Chennai
Dar es Salaam   Delhi   Hong Kong   Istanbul   Karachi   Kolkata
Kuala Lumpur   Madrid   Melbourne   Mexico City   Mumbai   Nairobi
São Paulo   Shanghai   Singapore   Taipei   Tokyo   Toronto

with an associated company in Berlin

OXFORD and OXFORD ENGLISH
are trade marks of Oxford University Press

ISBN 0 19 423008 2

Original edition copyright © 1970 by Erich Segal
This simplified edition © Oxford University Press 2000

Eighth impression 2002

First published in Oxford Bookworms 1990
This second edition published in the Oxford Bookworms Library 2000

A complete recording (in American English) of this Bookworms edition of
Love Story is available on cassette ISBN 0 19 422862 2

Photographs courtesy of Paramount Pictures
Love Story copyright © 1970 by Paramount Pictures Corporation
All Rights Reserved

The publisher has made every reasonable attempt
to obtain full clearance of film material, and will make
an appropriate payment in the event of any oversight.

Printed in Spain by Unigraf s.l.

CONTENTS

1

Stupid and rich, clever and poor

WHAT can you say about a twenty-five-year-old girl who died?

You can say that she was beautiful and intelligent. She loved Mozart and Bach and the Beatles. And me. Once, when she told me that, I asked her who came first. She answered, smiling, 'Like in the ABC.' I smiled too. But now I wonder. Was she talking about my first name? If she was, I came last, behind Mozart. Or did she mean my last name? If she did, I came between Bach and the Beatles. But I still didn't come first. That worries me terribly now. You see, I always had to be Number One. Family pride, you see.

In the autumn of my last year at Harvard University, I studied a lot in the Radcliffe library.

The library was quiet, nobody knew me there, and they had the books that I needed for my studies. The day before an examination I went over to the library desk to ask for a book. Two girls were working there. One was tall and sporty. The other was quiet and wore glasses. I chose her, and asked for my book.

She gave me an unfriendly look. 'Don't you have a library at Harvard?' she asked.

'Radcliffe let us use their library,' I answered.

'Yes, Preppie, they do – but is it fair? Harvard has five million books. We have a few thousand.'

Oh dear, I thought. A clever Radcliffe girl. I can usually make girls like her feel very small. But I needed that damn book, so I had to be polite.

'Listen, I need that damn book.'

'Don't speak like that to a lady, Preppie.'

'Why are you so sure that I went to prep school?'

She took off her glasses. 'You look stupid and rich,' she said.

'You're wrong,' I said. 'I'm actually clever and poor.'

'Oh no, Preppie,' she said. '*I'm* clever and poor.'

She was looking straight at me. All right, she had pretty brown eyes; and OK, perhaps I looked rich. But I don't let anyone call me stupid.

'What makes you so clever?' I asked.

'I'm not going to go for coffee with you,' she said.

'Listen – I'm not going to ask you!'

'That', she said, 'is what makes you stupid.'

Let me explain why I took her for coffee. I got the book that I wanted, didn't I? And she couldn't leave the library until closing time. So I was able to study the book for a good long time. I got an A in my exam the next day.

I gave the girl's legs an A too, when she came out from behind the library desk. We went to a coffee shop and I ordered coffee for both of us.

'I'm Jennifer Cavilleri,' she said. 'I'm American, but my family came from Italy. I'm studying music.'

'My name is Oliver,' I said.

'Is that your first or your last name?' she asked.

'I'm not going to go for coffee with you,' she said.

'First. My other name is Barrett.'

'Oh,' she said. 'Like Elizabeth Barrett the writer?'

'Yes,' I said. 'No relation.'

I was pleased that she hadn't said, 'Barrett, like Barrett Hall?' That Barrett *is* a relation of mine. Barrett Hall is a large, unlovely building at Harvard University. My great-grandfather gave it to Harvard long ago, and I am deeply ashamed of it.

She was silent. She sat there, half-smiling at me. I looked at her notebooks.

'Sixteenth-century music?' I said. 'That sounds difficult.'

'It's too difficult for you, Preppie,' she said coldly.

Why was I letting her talk to me like this? Didn't she read

3

the university magazine? Didn't she know who I was?

'Hey, don't you know who I am?'

'Yes,' she answered. 'You're the man who owns Barrett Hall.'

She didn't know who I was.

'I don't *own* Barrett Hall,' I argued. 'My great-grandfather gave it to Harvard, that's all.'

'So that's why his not-so-great grandson could get into Harvard so easily!'

I was angry now. 'Jenny, if I'm no good, why did you want me to invite you for coffee?'

She looked straight into my eyes and smiled.

'I like your body,' she said.

Every big winner has to be a good loser too. Every good Harvard man knows that. But it's better if you can win. And so, as I walked with Jenny to her dormitory, I made my winning move.

'Listen, Friday night is the Dartmouth hockey match.'

'So?'

'So I'd like you to come.'

These Radcliffe girls, they really care about sport. 'And why', she asked, 'should I come to a stupid ice-hockey match?'

'Because I'm playing,' I answered.

There was a moment's silence. I think I heard snow falling.

'For which team?' she said.

* * *

4

By the second quarter of the game on Friday night, we were winning 0 – 0. That is, Davey Johnson and I were getting ready to score a goal. The crowd were screaming for blood – or a goal. I always feel that it's my job to give them both these things. I didn't look up at Jenny once, but I hoped she was watching me.

I got the puck and started off across the ice. Davey Johnson was there on my left, but I didn't pass the puck to him. I wanted to score this goal myself. But before I could shoot, two big Dartmouth men were after me. In a moment we were hitting the puck and each other as hard as we could.

In a moment we were hitting the puck and each other as hard as we could.

5

'You!' said a voice suddenly. 'Two minutes in the penalty box.'

I looked up. He was talking to me. 'What did I do?' I asked.

'Don't argue.' He called to the officials' desk: 'Number seven, two minutes in the penalty box, for fighting.'

Angrily I climbed into the penalty box.

'Why are you sitting here when all your friends are playing?'

The voice was Jenny's. I didn't answer. 'Come on, Harvard, get that puck!' I shouted.

'What did you do wrong?' Jenny asked.

'I tried too hard.' Out there on the ice Harvard were playing with only five men.

'Is that something to be ashamed of?'

'Jenny, please. I'm thinking.'

'What about?'

'About those two Dartmouth men. When I get back onto the ice, I'll break them into little pieces.'

'Do you always fight when you play hockey?'

'I'll fight you, Jenny, if you don't keep quiet.'

'I'm leaving. Goodbye.'

I looked round, but she had gone. Just then the bell rang. My two-minute penalty had finished. I jumped onto the ice again.

'Good old Barrett!' shouted the crowd. Jenny will hear them shouting for me, I thought. But where was she? Had she left?

As I went for the puck, I looked up into the crowd. Jenny

'Do you always fight when you play hockey?' asked Jenny.

was standing there. I took the puck and went towards the goal line. Two Dartmouth players were coming straight at me.

'Go, Oliver, go! Knock their heads off!'

That was Jenny's voice above the crowd. It was crazily, beautifully violent. I pushed past one Dartmouth man. I knocked hard into the other. Then I passed the puck to Davey Johnson, and he banged it into the Dartmouth goal. The crowd went wild.

In a moment we were all shouting and kissing and banging each other on the back. The crowd were screaming with

7

'Go, Oliver, go! Knock their heads off!'

excitement. After that, we murdered Dartmouth – seven goals to zero.

After the match I lay in the hot bath and thought with pride about the game. I'd scored one goal, and helped to score another. Now the water felt wonderful on my tired body. Ahhhh!

Suddenly I remembered Jenny. Was she still waiting outside? I hoped so! I jumped out of that bath and dressed as fast as I could.

Outside, the cold winter air hit me. I looked round for Jenny. Had she walked back to her dormitory alone? Suddenly I saw her.

'Hey, Preppie, it's cold out here.'

I was really pleased to see her, and gave her a quick kiss.

'Did I say you could kiss me?' she said.

'Sorry. I was just excited.'

'I wasn't.'

It was dark and quiet, out there in the cold. I kissed her again, more slowly. When we reached her dormitory, I did not kiss her goodnight.

'Listen, Jenny, perhaps I won't telephone you for a few months.'

She was silent for a moment. 'Why?' she asked at last.

'But perhaps I'll telephone you as soon as I get back to my dorm.' I turned and began to walk away.

'Damn Preppie!' I heard her say. I turned again. From twenty feet away I scored another goal.

'You see, Jenny, that's the kind of thing *you* say. And when other people do it to you, you don't like it.'

I wished I could see the look on her face. But I couldn't look back. My pride wouldn't let me.

When I returned to my dorm, Ray Stratton was there. He and I slept in the same room. Ray was playing cards with some of his football-playing friends.

'Hullo, Ollie,' said Ray. 'How many goals did you score?'

'I scored one, and I made one,' I answered.

'With Cavilleri?'

'That's none of your business!' I replied quickly.

'Who's Cavilleri?' asked one of the footballers.

'Jenny Cavilleri. Studies music. Plays the piano with the Music Group.'

'What does she play with Barrett?' Everyone laughed.

'Get lost!' I said as I entered my room.

There I took off my shoes, lay back on my bed and telephoned Jenny's dormitory.

'Hey, Jen . . .' I said softly.

'Yes?'

'I think I'm in love with you.'

She was silent for a few moments. Then she answered, very softly: 'Oliver, you're crazy.'

I wasn't unhappy. Or surprised.

2

Blood and stone

A FEW weeks later I was hurt in the hockey match at Cornell university. My face was badly cut and the officials gave me the penalty for starting the fight. Five minutes! I sat quietly in the penalty box while the team manager cleaned the blood off my face. I was ashamed to look out onto the ice. But the shouts of the crowd told me everything. Cornell scored a goal. The score was 3–3 now. Damn, I thought. We're going to lose this match, because of me.

Across the ice, among the crowd, I saw him. My father. Old Stonyface. He was looking straight at me.

'*If the meeting finishes in time, I'll come to Cornell and watch you play*,' he had told me on the phone.

And there he was, Oliver Barrett the Third. What was he thinking about? Who could say? Why was he here? Family pride, perhaps. '*Look at me. I am a very busy, important man, but I have come all the way to Cornell, just to watch my son play in a hockey match*.'

We lost, six goals to three. After the match the doctor put twelve stitches in my face.

When I got to the changing-room, it was empty. They don't want to talk to me, I thought. *I* lost that match. I felt very ashamed as I walked out into the winter night.

'Come and have dinner, son,' said a voice. It was Old Stonyface.

At dinner we had one of our non-conversations. We spoke

11

'Come and have dinner, son,' said Old Stonyface after the match.

to each other, but didn't actually *say* anything. These non-conversations always started with 'How have you been, son?' and ended with 'Is there anything I can do for you?'

'How have you been, son?' my father began.

'Fine, sir.'

'Does your face hurt?'

'No, sir.' (It hurt terribly.)

Next, Old Stonyface talked about Playing the Game. 'All right, son, you lost the match.' (How clever of you to notice, Father.) 'But after all, in sport, the important thing is the playing, not the winning.'

Wonderful, I thought. Father was chosen for the Olympic Games. And now he says winning is not important!

I just looked down at my plate and said 'Yes, sir' at the right times.

Our non-conversation continued. After Playing the Game, he discussed My Plans.

'Tell me, Oliver, has the Law School accepted you yet?'

'Not yet, sir.'

'Would you like me to telephone them?'

'No!' I said at once. 'I want to get a letter like other people, sir. Please.'

'Yes, of course. Fine . . . After all, they're sure to accept *you*.'

Why? I thought. Because I'm clever and successful? Or because I'm the son of Oliver Barrett the Third?

The meal was as uninteresting as the conversation. At last my father spoke again.

'There's always the Peace Corps,' he said suddenly. 'I

think the Peace Corps is a fine thing, don't you?'

'Oh, yes, sir,' I said politely. I knew nothing about the Peace Corps.

'What do your friends at Harvard think about the Peace Corps?' he asked. 'Do they feel that the Peace Corps is important in our world today?'

'Yes, sir,' I said politely, just to please him.

After dinner I walked with him to his car.

'Is there anything I can do for you, son?' he asked.

'No, thank you, sir. Good night, sir.'

Our non-conversation was finished: he drove away. Yes, of course there are planes, but Oliver Barrett the Third chose to drive. My father likes to drive – fast. And at that time of night, in an Aston Martin DBS, you can go very fast indeed.

I went to telephone Jenny. That was the only good part of the evening. I told her about the fight. She enjoyed that. Her musical friends never got into fights.

'I hope you hit the man who hit you,' she said.

'Oh, yes.'

'Good! I'm sorry I couldn't be there to watch you. Perhaps you'll hit somebody in the Yale match?'

I smiled. Jenny really made me feel better.

Back at Harvard the next day I called at her dorm. Jenny was talking to someone on the telephone in the hall.

'Yes. Of course! Oh yes, Phil. I love you too. Love and kisses. Goodbye.'

Who was she talking to? I had only been away forty-eight

hours, and she had found a new boyfriend!

Jenny did not seem ashamed. She kissed me lightly on the unhurt side of my face.

'Hey – you look terrible!'

'Twelve stitches, Jen.'

'Does the other man look worse than you?'

'Much worse. I always make the other man look worse.'

We walked to my MG sports car. 'Who's Phil?' I asked as carelessly as I could.

'My father.'

I could not believe that! 'You call your father Phil?'

'That's his name. What do you call *your* father?'

'Sir.'

'He must be really proud of you. You're a big hockey star – *and* you're always successful in your exams.'

'You don't know anything, Jenny. He was good at exams and sport, too. He was in the Olympic Games.'

'My God! Did he win?'

'No.' (Actually, Old Stonyface was sixth, which makes me feel a little better.)

Jenny was silent for a moment.

'Why do you hate him so much?' she asked at last.

'I'm Oliver Barrett the Fourth,' I answered. 'All Barretts have to be successful. And that means I have to be good at everything, all the time. I hate it.'

'Oh, I'm sure you do,' laughed Jenny. 'You hate doing well in your exams. You hate being a hockey star . . .'

'But he *expects* it!' I said. 'If I'm successful, he isn't

excited, or surprised. He was a big success, and he expects me to be the same.'

I told her about our meal and our non-conversation after the Cornell match, but she didn't understand at all.

'You say your father is a busy man,' she said. 'But he found time to go all the way to Cornell to watch you play. How can you say these terrible things about him, when he drove all that way, just to watch your hockey match? He loves you, Oliver – can't you understand?'

'Forget it, Jenny,' I said. She was silent for a moment.

'I'm pleased you have problems with your father,' she said at last. 'That means you aren't perfect.'

'Oh – you mean you *are* perfect?'

'Of course not, Preppie. That's why I go out with you!'

Jenny loved to have the last word.

3

We belong together

I HAD not yet made love to Jenny. In the three weeks we had been together, we had held hands. Sometimes we had kissed, but that was all. Usually I moved much faster – ask the other girls that I'd been out with! But Jenny was special. I felt different about her and I didn't know what to say to her.

'You're going to fail your exams, Oliver.'

We were studying in my room one Sunday afternoon.

'Oliver, you'll fail your exams if you don't do some work.'

'I *am* working.'

'No, you aren't. You're looking at my legs.'

'Only once every chapter.'

'That book has very short chapters.'

'Listen, you aren't as good-looking as all that!'

'I know, but *you* think I am, don't you?'

'Dammit, Jenny, how can I study when all the time I want to make love to you?'

She closed her book softly and put it down. She put her arms around me.

'Oliver, will you please make love to me?'

It all happened at once. It was all so unhurried, soft and gentle. And *I* was gentle too. Was this the real Oliver Barrett the Fourth?

'Hey, Oliver, did I ever tell you that I love you?' said Jenny finally.

'No, Jen.' I kissed her neck.

Sometimes we had kissed, but that was all.

'I love you very much, Oliver.'

I love Ray Stratton too. He's not very clever, or a wonderful footballer, but he was a good friend to me. Where did he go to study when I was in our room with Jenny? Where did he sleep on those Saturdays when Jenny and I spent the night together? In the old days I always told him all about my girlfriends. But I never told him about Jenny and me.

'My God, Barrett, are you two sleeping together or not?' asked Ray.

'Raymond, please don't ask.'

'You spend every minute of your free time with her. It isn't natural . . .'

'Ray, when two adults are in love . . .'

'Love? At your age? My God, I worry about you, I really do.'

'Don't worry, Raymond, old friend. We'll have that flat in New York one day. Different girls every night . . .'

'Don't you tell me not to worry, Barrett. That girl's *got* you, and I don't like it!'

That evening I went to hear Jenny play the piano with the Music Group.

'You were wonderful,' I said afterwards.

'That shows what you know about music, Preppie.' We walked along the river together. 'I played OK. Not wonderful. Not "Olympic Games". Just OK. OK?'

'OK – but you should always continue your music.'

'Of course I will. I'm going to study with Nadia Boulanger, aren't I?'

19

'Who?'

'Nadia Boulanger. She's a famous music teacher in Paris. I'm very lucky. I won a scholarship, too.'

'Jennifer – you're going to Paris?'

'I've never seen Europe. I'm really excited about it.'

I took her by the arms and pulled her towards me. 'Hey – how long have you known this?'

Jenny looked down at her feet. 'Oliver, don't be stupid. We can't do anything about it. After we finish university, you'll go your way and I'll go mine. You'll go to law school—'

'Wait a minute! What are you talking about?'

She looked into my eyes. 'Ollie, you're a rich Preppie. Your old man owns a bank. My father's a baker in Cranston, Rhode Island . . . and I'm nobody.'

'What does that matter? We're together now. We're happy.'

'Ollie, don't be stupid,' she repeated. 'Harvard is full of all kinds of different people. You study together, you have fun together. But afterwards you have to go back to where you belong.'

'We belong together. Don't leave me, Jenny. Please.'

'What about my scholarship? What about Paris?'

'What about our marriage?'

'Who said anything about marriage?' said Jenny in surprise.

'Me. I'm saying it now.'

'Why?'

I looked straight into her eyes.

'*After we finish university, you'll go your way and I'll go mine.*'

'Because,' I said.

'Oh,' said Jenny. 'That's a very good reason.' She took my arm and we walked along the river. There was nothing more to say, really.

The next Sunday we drove to visit my parents in Ipswich, Massachusetts. Jenny said it was the right thing to do, and of course there was also the fact that Oliver the Third paid for my studies at Harvard.

'Oh my God,' Jenny said when we drove up to the house. 'I didn't expect this. It's like a damn palace!'

'Please, Jen. Everything will be fine.'

'For a nice all-American girl of good family, perhaps. Not for Jennifer Cavilleri, baker's daughter, from Cranston, Rhode Island.'

Florence opened the door. She has worked for the Barrett family for many years. She told us that my parents were waiting in the library. We followed her past a long line of pictures of famous Barretts and a glass case full of silver and gold cups.

'They look just like real silver and gold,' said Jenny. 'They don't give cups like those at the Cranston Sports Club!'

'They *are* real silver and gold,' I answered.

'My God! Are they yours?'

'No, my father's.'

'Do you have silver and gold cups too, Oliver?'

'Yes.'

'In a glass case, like these?'

'No. Up in my room, under the bed.'

She gave me one of her good Jenny-looks. 'We'll go and look at them later, shall we?'

Before I could answer, we heard a voice.

'Ah, hello there.' It was Old Stonyface.

'Oh, hello, sir. This is Jennifer—'

'Hello there.' He shook her hand before I could say her full name. There was a smile on his usually rock-like face. 'Do come in and meet Mrs Barrett . . . My wife Alison. This is Jennifer—'

'Calliveri,' I said – for the first and only time, I got her damn name wrong!

'Cavilleri,' said Jenny politely. Mother and Jenny shook hands.

All through dinner Mother kept the polite small talk going.

'So your people are from Cranston, Jennifer?' said my mother.

'Mostly. My mother came from Fall River.'

'The Barretts have factories at Fall River,' said Oliver the Third.

'Where they cheated their workers for centuries,' said Oliver the Fourth.

'In the nineteenth century,' said Oliver the Third.

'What about the plans to put automatic machines in the factories?' said Oliver the Fourth.

'What about coffee?' my mother said quickly. We moved back into the library. We sat there with nothing to say to each other. So I started a new non-conversation.

'Tell me, Jennifer,' I said, 'what do you think about the Peace Corps?' She looked at me in surprise.

'Oh, have you told them, O.B.?' asked my mother.

'It isn't the time for that, my dear,' said Oliver Barrett the Third, with an 'Ask me, ask me!' look on his face.

'What's this, Father?' I asked, just to please him.

'Nothing important, son.'

'I don't know how you can say that,' said my mother. She turned to me. 'Your father is going to be Head of the Peace Corps.'

'Oh,' I said.

'Oh!' said Jenny in a different, happier kind of voice. 'Well done, Mr Barrett.' She gave me a hard look.

'Yes. Well done, sir,' I said at last.

Jenny gave me a hard look across the table.

4

Two different kinds of father

'JENNY, he isn't going to be President of the USA, after all!' We were driving back to Harvard.

'You still weren't very nice to him about it, Oliver.'

'I said "Well done"!'

'Ha! Oliver, why are you so unkind to your father? You hurt him all the time.'

'It's impossible to hurt Oliver Barrett the Third.'

'No, it isn't – if you marry Jennifer Cavilleri . . . Oliver, I know you love me. But in a strange way you want me because I'm not a suitable woman for a Barrett to marry. You are rebelling against your father.'

My father said the same thing a few days later when we had lunch together at the Harvard Club in Boston.

'Son, you're in too much of a hurry. The young lady herself is fine. The problem is *you*. You are rebelling, and you know it.'

'Father, what worries you most about her? That she's Italian? Or that she's poor?'

'What do you *like* most about her?'

'I'm leaving.'

'Stay and talk like a man.' I stayed. Old Stonyface liked that. He's won again, I thought angrily.

'Wait a while, son,' Oliver Barrett the Third continued. 'That's all I ask. Finish law school.'

'Why do I have to wait?' I was rebelling now.

'Oliver, you are still under twenty-one. In the eyes of the law you are not yet an adult.'

'Stop talking like a lawyer, dammit!'

'If you marry her now, you will get nothing from me.'

'Father, you've got nothing that I want.'

I walked out of his club and out of his life.

After that, I was not looking forward to meeting Jenny's father. She was his only child and her mother was dead. She meant a lot to him . . . I could see a lot of problems there. *And* I was penniless. How is Mr Cavilleri going to feel, I thought, when he hears that young Barrett can't support his daughter? Worse, she will have to work as a teacher to support him while he is at law school!

As we drove down to Cranston on that Sunday in May, I worried a lot about Mr Cavilleri's feelings.

'Tell me again, Jen.'

'OK. I telephoned him, and he said OK.'

'But what does he *mean* by "OK"?'

'Are you trying to tell me that Harvard Law School has accepted a man who doesn't know the meaning of "OK"?'

'It isn't a word that lawyers use much, Jen. Just tell me again. Please.'

'He knows you're poor, and he doesn't mind. Stop worrying, Oliver.'

Jenny lived on Hamilton Street. It was a long line of wooden houses with children playing in front of them, and whole families sitting on their front steps. I felt like a stranger in a strange land as I parked the MG outside 189A Hamilton Street. Mr Cavilleri's handshake was warm and strong.

'How do you do, sir?' I said.

'I'm Phil,' he said.

'Phil, sir.' It was a frightening moment. Then Mr Cavilleri turned to his daughter. Suddenly they were in each other's arms, laughing and crying and kissing. I felt like a stranger.

For some time I did not have to speak much. 'Don't speak with your mouth full,' my family had told me when I was a child. Phil and his daughter kept my mouth full all afternoon. I don't know how many Italian cakes I ate. Both Cavilleris were very pleased.

'He's OK,' said Phil at last.

'I told you he was OK,' said his daughter.

'Well, I had to see for myself. Now I've seen him. Oliver—'

'Yes, sir?'

'Call me Phil. You're OK.'

Later Phil tried to have a serious talk with me. He thought he could bring Oliver Barrett the Third and Oliver Barrett the Fourth together again.

'Let me speak to him on the telephone,' he said. 'A father's love is a very special thing . . .'

'There isn't much of it in my family,' I said.

'Your father will soon realize,' he began. 'When it's time to go to the church—'

'Phil,' said Jenny gently, 'we don't want to be married in church.'

He looked surprised, then unhappy. But he spoke bravely.

'Call me Phil,' said Mr Cavilleri. 'Oliver, you're OK.'

'It's your wedding, children. You choose. It's OK by me.'

My next meeting was with the Head of Harvard Law School.
    'I'll need a scholarship for next year, sir,' I said politely.
    'A scholarship? I don't understand. Your father—'
    'My father has nothing to do with it, sir. We've had a disagreement, and he isn't supporting me any more.' The Head took off his glasses, then put them on again. I continued, 'That's why I've come here to see you, sir. I'm getting married next month. We're both going to work during the summer. Then Jenny will support us by teaching. But her teaching won't pay enough to send me to law school. Sir, I need a scholarship. I have no money in the bank.'
    'Mr Barrett, our scholarships are for poor people. And it's too late to ask for one. I do not wish to enter into a family disagreement, but I think you should go and talk to your father again.'
    'Oh no!' I said angrily. 'I am not, repeat *not,* going back to my father to ask for money!'

When Jenny graduated from university that summer, all her relations came from Cranston to watch. We didn't tell them about our marriage plans because we wanted a quiet wedding, and didn't want to hurt their feelings. I graduated from Harvard the next day. Was Oliver the Third there in the university hall? I don't know. I didn't look for Old Stonyface in the crowd. I gave my parents' tickets to Jenny and Phil, but as an old Harvard man my father could sit with

'I think you should go and talk to your father again.'

the Class of '26. But why should he want to? I mean, weren't the banks open that day?

The wedding was on the next Sunday. It was very quiet and very beautiful. Phil was there, of course, and my friend Ray Stratton. Jenny and I spoke about our love for each other and promised to stay together until death. Ray gave me the ring and soon Oliver Barrett the Fourth and Jennifer Cavilleri were man and wife.

We had a small party afterwards, just the four of us. Then Ray and Phil went home and Jenny and I were alone together.

'Jenny, we're really married!'

'Yes. Now I can be as terrible to you as I like!'

Our wedding was very quiet and very beautiful.

5

The first three years

FOR three years we had to make every dollar do the work of two. All through the summer holidays we worked at the Boat Club in Dennis Port. It was hard work, but we were never too tired to be kind to each other. I say 'kind' because there are no words to describe our love and happiness together.

After the summer we found a 'cheap' flat near the university. It was on the top floor of an old house and was actually very expensive. But what could we do? There weren't many flats around.

'Hey, Preppie,' said Jenny when we arrived there. 'Are you my husband or aren't you?'

'Of course I'm your husband.'

'Show me, then.' (My God, I thought, in the street?) 'Carry me into our first home!'

I carried her up the five steps to the front door.

'Why did you stop?' she asked. 'This isn't our home. Upstairs, Preppie!'

There were twenty-four stairs up to our flat, and I had to stop half-way.

'Why are you so heavy?' I asked her.

'Perhaps I'm expecting a baby.'

'My God! Are you?'

'Ha! I frightened you then, didn't I?'

'Well, yes, just for a second or two.'

I carried her the rest of the way. There were very few

'Carry me into our first home!'

moments in those days when we were not worrying about money. Very few, and very wonderful – and that moment was one of them.

A food shop let us 'eat now, pay later', thanks to the Barrett name. But our famous name did not help us in Jenny's work. The Head of the school thought we were rich.

'Of course, we can't pay our teachers very much,' said Miss Whitman. 'But that won't worry *you*, Mrs Barrett!'

Jenny tried to explain that Barretts had to eat, just like other people. Miss Whitman just laughed politely.

'Don't worry,' Jenny said to me. 'We'll manage. Just learn to like spaghetti.'

I did. I learned to like spaghetti and Jenny learned lots of different ways of cooking it. With Jenny's pay from school, and our money from our summer work and my holiday jobs, we managed. Our lives had changed a lot, of course. There was no more music for Jenny. She had to teach all day, and came home very tired. Then she had to cook dinner – restaurants were too expensive for us. There were a lot of films that we didn't see, and places and people that we didn't visit. But we were doing OK.

One day a beautiful invitation arrived. It was for my father's sixtieth birthday party.

'Well?' said Jenny. I was in the middle of a thick law book and did not hear her at first. 'Oliver, he's reaching out to you.'

'No, he isn't. My mother wrote it. Now be quiet. I'm studying. I've got exams in three weeks.'

'Ollie, think. Sixty years old, dammit. How do you know that he'll still be alive when *you* decide to forget your disagreement?'

'I don't know, and I don't care. Now let me get on with my work!'

'One day,' said Jenny, 'when you're having problems with Oliver the Fifth—'

'Our son won't be called Oliver, you can be sure of that!' I said angrily.

'You can call him Bozo if you like. But that child will feel bad about you, because you were a big Harvard sportsman. And by the time he goes to university, you'll probably be a big, important lawyer!' She continued, 'Oliver, your father loves you, in the same way as you will love Bozo. But you Barretts are so full of pride – you'll go through life thinking that you hate each other. Now . . . what about that invitation?'

'Write them a nice letter of refusal.'

'Oliver, I can't hurt your father like that . . . What's their telephone number?'

I told her and was at once deep in my law book again. I tried not to listen to her talking on the telephone, but she was in the same room, after all. Suddenly I thought, *How long does it take to say no?*

'Ollie?' Jenny had her hand over the telephone mouthpiece. 'Ollie, do we have to say no?'

'Yes, we do. And hurry up, dammit!'

'I'm terribly sorry,' she said into the telephone. She

covered the mouthpiece again and turned to me. 'He's very unhappy, Oliver! Can you just sit there and let your father bleed?'

'Stones don't bleed, Jen. This isn't one of your warm, loving Italian fathers.'

'Oliver, can't you just speak to him?'

'Speak to him! Are you crazy?'

She held the telephone towards me. She was trying not to cry.

'I will never speak to him. Ever,' I said.

Now she was crying, very quietly. Then she asked me once more. 'For me, Oliver. I've never asked you for anything. Please.'

I couldn't do it. Didn't Jenny understand? It was just impossible. Unhappily I shook my head. Then Jenny spoke to me quietly and very angrily. 'You have no heart,' she said.

She spoke into the telephone again. 'Mr Barrett, Oliver wants you to know . . . ' She was crying, so it wasn't easy for her. 'Oliver loves you very much,' she said, and put the telephone down quickly.

I don't know why I did it. Perhaps I went crazy for a moment. Violently I took the telephone and threw it across the room.

'Damn you, Jenny! Why don't you get out of my life?'

I stood still for a second. My God, I thought, what's happening to me? I turned to look at Jenny. But she had gone.

I looked round the flat for her. Her coat was still there, but she had disappeared.

Where, oh where, had Jenny gone?

I ran out of the house and searched everywhere for her: the law school library, Radcliffe, the music school. Was she in one of the music rooms? I heard somebody playing the piano, loudly and very badly. Was it Jenny? I pushed the door open. A big Radcliffe girl was at the piano.

'What's the matter?' she asked.

'Nothing,' I answered, and closed the door again.

Where, oh where, had she gone? I felt terrible. I searched the university, the streets and the cafés. Nothing. Had she taken a bus to Cranston, perhaps? At midnight I found a telephone box and called Phil.

'Hello?' he said sleepily. 'What's the matter? Is Jenny ill?'

My God, I thought, she isn't there! 'She's fine, Phil. Uh – I just called to say hello.'

'You should call more often, dammit,' he said. 'Is Cranston so far away that you can't come down on a Sunday afternoon?'

'We'll come, some Sunday, Phil, I promise.'

'Don't give me that – "some Sunday" indeed! *This* Sunday, Oliver.'

'Yes, sir. This Sunday.'

'And next time you telephone, I'll pay, dammit. OK?' He put down the telephone. I stood there and wondered what to do. At last I went back to the flat.

Jenny was sitting on the top step. I was too tired to cry, too glad to speak.

'I forgot my key,' said Jenny.

I stood there on the bottom step. I was afraid to ask how

long she had been there. I only knew that I had hurt her terribly.

'Jenny, I'm sorry—'

'Stop!' she said. Then she added, 'Love means you never have to say you're sorry.'

We walked up to our flat. As we undressed, she looked lovingly at me.

'I meant what I said, Oliver.'

And that was all.

6

Money can't buy everything

WHEN the letter came from the Law School, it changed our lives. I came third in the final examinations and suddenly everyone wanted to offer me jobs. It was a wonderful time. Think of it: an all-American boy with a famous name, third in his examinations and a Harvard hockey player too. Crowds of people were fighting to get my name and number on their company writing paper.

At last I accepted a job with Jonas and Marsh in New York. I was the highest-paid graduate of my year too. After three years of spaghetti and looking twice at every dollar, it felt wonderful.

We moved to a beautiful flat in New York. Jonas and Marsh's office was an easy ten-minute walk away. And there were lots of fashionable shops nearby too. I told my wife to get in there and start spending immediately.

'Why, Oliver?'

'Woman, you supported me for three years. Now it's my turn!'

I joined the Harvard Club of New York. Ray Stratton was working in New York too and we played tennis together three times a week. My old Harvard friends discovered me once more, and invitations arrived.

'Say no, Oliver. I don't want to spend my free time with a lot of empty-headed preppies.'

'OK, Jen, but what shall I tell them?'

We moved to a beautiful flat in New York.

'Tell them I'm expecting a baby.'

'Are you?'

She smiled. 'No, but if we stay at home tonight, perhaps I will.'

We already had a name for our child.

'You know,' I said one evening. 'I really like the name Bozo.'

'You honestly want to call our child Bozo?'

'Yes. It's the name of a big sports star. He'll be wonderfully big and strong,' I continued. 'Bozo Barrett, Harvard's biggest football star.'

We had a name for our child and we wanted him very much. But it's not always easy to make a baby, although we tried

41

very hard. Finally I became worried and we went together to see a doctor.

Doctor Sheppard checked everything carefully. He took some of our blood and sent it away for examination. 'We'll know soon,' he said.

A few days later he telephoned me at my office and asked me to visit him on my way home that evening.

'Well, Doctor,' I said, 'which of us has the problem?'

'It's Jenny,' he said. 'She will never have children.'

I was ready for this news, but it still shook me. 'Well,' I said, 'children aren't everything.'

'Oliver,' said Doctor Sheppard, 'the problem is more serious than that. Jenny is very ill. She has a blood disease. It is destroying her blood, and we can't stop it. She is dying, Oliver. I am very sorry.'

'That's impossible, Doctor,' I said. I waited for the doctor to tell me that it was not true.

Kindly and patiently he explained again, and at last I understood the terrible words.

'Have you spoken to Jenny, Doctor? What did you tell her?'

'I told her that you were both all right. For the moment it's better that way.'

I wanted to shout and scream at the unfairness of it all. Jenny was twenty-four, and she was dying. 'What can I do to help, Doctor?' I asked at last.

'Just be natural,' he said. *Natural!*

I began to think about God. At first I hated Him. Then next morning I woke up and Jenny was there beside me. Still

I waited for the doctor to tell me that it was not true.

there. I was ashamed. Thank you, God, I thought. Thank you for letting me wake up and see Jennifer.

'Be natural,' the doctor had said. I did my best, and all the time I was living with my terrible secret.

One day Mr Jonas called me into his office. 'Oliver, I have an important job for you. How soon can you go to Chicago? You can take one of the younger men with you.'

One of the younger men? I was the youngest man in the office. I understood the message: Oliver, although you are still only twenty-four, you are one of our top men.

'Thank you, sir,' I said, 'but I can't leave New York just now.'

I had decided not to tell anyone about my troubles. I wanted to keep my secret as long as possible. I could see that old man Jonas was unhappy about my refusal.

On the way home that day I saw a notice in a travel shop window: 'Fly to Paris!' Suddenly I remembered Jenny's words: *What about my scholarship? What about Paris?*

I went into the shop and bought two tickets to Paris.

Jenny was looking grey and tired when I got home. When I showed her the tickets, she shook her head.

'Oliver,' she said gently, 'I don't want Paris. I just want you . . . and I want time, which you can't give me.'

Now I looked in her eyes and saw the sadness in them. We sat there silently, holding each other. Then Jenny explained.

'I was feeling terrible. I went back to the doctor and he told me. I'm dying.'

Now I didn't have to be 'natural' any more. We had no

We sat there silently, holding each other.

more secrets from each other. Now we could discuss things . . . things that young husbands and wives don't usually have to discuss.

'You must be strong, Oliver,' she said. 'For Phil. It's going to be hard for him. He needs your help. OK?'

'OK. I'll be strong,' I promised. I hoped Jenny could not see how frightened I was.

A month later, just after dinner, Jenny was playing Chopin on the piano. Suddenly she stopped.

'Are you rich enough to pay for a taxi?' she asked.

'Of course. Where do you want to go?'

'To the hospital.'

In the next few busy, worried moments, while I hurriedly packed a bag, I realized. This is it, I thought. Jenny is going to walk out of this flat and never come back. I wondered what she was thinking. She sat there, looking straight in front of her.

'Hey,' I said, 'is there anything special that you want to take with you?'

'No,' she said. Then she thought again. 'Yes. You.'

The taxi-driver thought Jenny was expecting a baby. 'Is this your first?' he asked.

I was holding Jenny in my arms, and I felt ready to explode.

'Please, Ollie,' Jenny said to me softly. 'He's trying to be nice to us.'

'Yes,' I told the driver. 'It's our first. And my wife isn't feeling very well. So can you hurry, please?'

He got us to the hospital in ten minutes. 'Good luck!' he called as he drove away. Jenny thanked him.

She was having trouble walking. I wanted to carry her. But she said clearly, 'Not this time, Preppie.' So we walked.

'Have you got health insurance?' they asked us in the hospital.

'No.' We had never thought about buying insurance. We were too busy buying furniture and kitchen things.

Of course, the doctors knew about Jenny and they were expecting us.

'Listen,' I told them. 'Do your best for Jenny I don't care what it costs. I want her to have the best, please. I've got the money.'

7

Strong men don't cry

I JUMPED into my MG and drove through the night to Boston. I changed my shirt in the car before I entered the offices on State Street. It was only eight o'clock in the morning, but several important-looking people were waiting to see Oliver Barrett the Third. His secretary recognized me and spoke my name into the telephone. My father did not say 'Show him in'. Instead, the door opened and he came out to meet me.

'Oliver,' he said. His hair was a little greyer and his face had lost some of its colour. 'Come in, son,' he said. I walked into his office and sat down opposite him.

For a moment we looked at each other. Then he looked away, and so did I. I looked at the things on his desk: the scissors, the pen-holder, the letter-opener, the photos of my mother and me.

'How have you been, son?' he asked.

'Very well, sir . . . Father, I need to borrow five thousand dollars.'

He looked hard at me. 'May I know the reason?' he said at last.

'I can't tell you, Father. Just lend me the money. Please.'

I felt that he didn't want to refuse, or argue with me. He wanted to give me the money, but he also wanted to . . . talk.

'Don't they pay you at Jonas and Marsh?'

'Yes, sir.' So he knows where I work, I thought. He

'Father, I need to borrow five thousand dollars.'

probably knows how much they pay me too.

'And doesn't Jennifer teach too?' Well, I thought, he doesn't know everything.

'Please leave Jennifer out of this, Father. This is a personal matter. A very important personal matter.'

'Have you got a girl into trouble?' he asked quietly.

'Yes,' I lied. 'That's it. Now give me the money. Please.'

I think he knew that I was lying. But I don't think he wanted to know my real reason for wanting the money. He was asking because he wanted to . . . talk.

He took out his cheque book and opened it slowly. Not

to hurt me, I'm sure, but to give himself time. Time to find things to say. Things that would not hurt the two of us.

He finished writing the cheque, took it out of the cheque book and held it out towards me. When I did not reach out my hand to take it, he pulled back his hand and placed the cheque on his desk. He looked at me again. Here it is, son, the look on his face seemed to say. But still he did not speak.

I did not want to leave, either. But I couldn't think of anything painless to say. And we couldn't sit there, wanting to talk but unable to look at each other.

I picked up the cheque and put it carefully into my shirt pocket. I got up and went towards the door. I wanted to thank my father for seeing me, when several important people were waiting outside his office. If I want, I thought, he will send his visitors away, just to be with me . . . I wanted to thank him for that, but the words refused to come. I stood there with the door half open, and at last I managed to look at him and say:

'Thank you, Father.'

Then I had to tell Phil Cavilleri. He did not cry or say anything. He quietly closed his house in Cranston and came to live in our flat. We all have ways of living with our troubles. Some people drink too much. Phil cleaned the flat, again and again. Perhaps he thought Jenny would come home again. Poor Phil.

Next I telephoned old man Jonas. I told him why I could not come into the office. I kept the conversation short

Then I had to tell Phil Cavilleri. He did not cry or say anything.

because I knew he was unhappy. He wanted to say things to me, but could not find the words. I knew all about that.

Phil and I lived for hospital visiting hours. The rest of life – eating and sleeping (or not sleeping) – meant nothing to us. One day, in the flat, I heard Phil saying, very quietly, 'I can't take this much longer.' I did not answer him. I just thought to myself, *I* can take it. Dear God, I can take it as long as You want – because Jenny is Jenny.

That evening, she sent me out of her room. She wanted

51

to speak to her father, 'man to man'. 'But don't go too far away,' she added.

I went to sit outside. Then Phil appeared. 'She wants to see you now,' he said.

'Close the door,' Jenny ordered. I went to sit by her bed. I always liked to sit beside her and look at her face, because it had her eyes shining in it.

'It doesn't hurt, Ollie, really,' she said. 'It's like falling off a high building very slowly – you know?'

Something moved deep inside me. I am *not* going to cry, I said to myself. I'm strong, OK? And strong men don't cry . . . But if I'm not going to cry, then I can't open my mouth. 'Mm,' I said.

'No, you don't know, Preppie,' she said. 'You've never fallen off a high building in your life.'

'Yes, I have.' My voice came back. 'I did when I met you.'

She smiled. 'Who cares about Paris?' she said suddenly. 'Paris, music, all that. You think you stole it from me, don't you? I can see it in your face. Well, I don't care, you stupid Preppie. Can't you accept that?'

'No,' I answered honestly.

'Then get out of here!' she said angrily. 'I don't want you at my damn death-bed.'

'OK, I accept it,' I said.

'That's better. Now – will you do something for me?' From somewhere inside me came this sudden, violent need to cry. But I was strong. I was *not* going to cry. 'Mm,' I said again.

'Will you please hold me, Oliver?'

'*Will you please hold me, Oliver?*'

I put my hand on her arm – oh God, she was so thin – and held it.

'No, Oliver,' she said. 'Really hold me. Put your arms round me.'

Very, very carefully I got onto the bed and put my arms round her.

'Thanks, Ollie.'

Those were her last words.

Phil Cavilleri was waiting outside. 'Phil?' I said softly. He looked up and I think he already knew. I walked over and put my hand on his arm.

'I won't cry,' he said quietly. 'I'm going to be strong for you. I promised Jenny.' He touched my hand very gently.

But I had to be alone. To feel the night air. To take a walk, perhaps.

Downstairs, the entrance hall of the hospital was very calm and quiet. The only noise was the sound of my footsteps on the hard floor.

'Oliver.'

It was my father. Except for the woman at the desk, we were all alone there. I could not speak to him. I went straight towards the door. But in a moment he was out there, standing beside me.

'Oliver,' he said. 'Why didn't you tell me?'

It was very cold. That was good, because I wanted to feel *something*. My father continued to speak to me, while I stood still and felt the cold wind on my face.

'Oliver,' said my father. 'I want to help.'

'I heard this evening. I jumped into the car at once.'

I was not wearing a coat. The cold was starting to make me ache. Good. Good.

'Oliver,' said my father. 'I want to help.'

'Jenny's dead,' I told him.

'I'm sorry,' he said very softly.

I don't know why I did it. But I repeated Jenny's words from long ago.

'Love means you never have to say you're sorry.'

Then I did something which I had never done in front of him before. My father put his arms round me, and I cried.

GLOSSARY

club a group of people with the same interests, and the building where they meet

damn/dammit words used to show that you are angry, disapproving, etc.

disagreement when people don't agree with each other

dormitory (dorm) a building where American university students sleep

examination (exam) a test, usually written in a short time, to show how much you know about something

expect to think that something will happen

God the 'person' who made the world and controls all things

graduate *(v)* to finish university successfully and pass your exams

hurt to make somebody feel unhappy

ice hockey a sport played on ice, using long sticks to hit a puck

insurance money paid each year to a company, which then pays your hospital bills, etc. if you are ill

kiss *(v)* to touch someone with your lips in a loving way

law the rules of a country, which all the people must obey

lawyer a person who has studied law

make love to sleep with (have sex with) someone

marriage when a man and a woman are married

Olympic Games the most famous sports meeting in the world, which happens every four years

Peace Corps an organization in the USA that sends young people to work in and help other countries

penalty the time a hockey player must spend out of the game because he has done something wrong

perfect without mistakes and excellent in every way

piano a large musical instrument with black and white keys

prep school an expensive private school for rich children

Preppie a word for a young man who has been to prep school

pride the feeling when you are pleased about something you are or have done

proud pleased about something you or other people have done

puck the round flat 'ball' used in ice hockey

rebel *(v)* to fight against what somebody has told you to do

relation a member of a family

scholarship money given to a clever person to pay for their studies

score *(v)* to get a goal, a point, etc. in a game or sport

stitch *(n)* a piece of thread that holds a cut together and stops it bleeding

support *(v)* to provide the money needed for someone's food, clothes, etc.

team a group of people who play a sport together, against another team

throw (past tense **threw**) to send something flying through the air

Love Story

ACTIVITIES

Before Reading

1 Read the back cover and the story introduction on the first page of the book. How much do you know now about Oliver and Jenny? For each sentence, circle Y (Yes) or N (No).

1 Oliver's family has more money than Jenny's. Y/N *y*
2 Jenny likes sport. Y/N *N*
3 They both play music. Y/N *N*
4 They are both clever. Y/N *y*
5 Oliver studies at Harvard University. Y/N *y*
6 Their fathers have the same kinds of job. Y/N *y*

2 Can you guess what will happen in the story? Choose Y (Yes) or N (No) for each sentence.

1 Oliver and Jenny are happy together. Y/N *y*
2 Oliver dies. Y/N *N*
3 Jenny dies. Y/N *y*
4 Oliver's father dies. Y/N *N*
5 Jenny's father dies. Y/N *N*
6 Oliver and Jenny have a baby. Y/N *N*
7 Oliver and Jenny are very poor. Y/N *y*
8 Jenny leaves Oliver. Y/N *y*
9 Oliver leaves Jenny. Y/N *y*
10 Oliver learns to love his father. Y/N *y*
11 The story has a happy ending. Y/N *N*

ACTIVITIES

While Reading

Read Chapter 1. These are the things that Oliver did in this chapter. Put them in the right order.

1 He took Jenny for a coffee.
2 He won the hockey match.
3 He asked Jenny for a book from the university library.
4 He invited Jenny to watch him play ice hockey.
5 He went back to his dorm.
6 He heard Jenny's voice in the crowd at the hockey match.
7 He phoned Jenny and said: 'I think I'm in love with you.'

Read Chapter 2. Match these halves of sentences, and join them together with these linking words.

that / why / although / because / so

1 Mr Barrett came to watch Oliver play hockey _so_
2 Oliver and his father often had 'non-conversations' _____
3 Oliver could not believe _____
4 Mr Barrett had always been successful in everything _____
5 Jenny did not understand _____
6 Jenny called her father 'Phil'.
7 he was a busy man.
8 Oliver hated his father so much.
9 they found it hard to talk about how they felt.
10 he expected Oliver to be the same.

61

Read Chapter 3, and then answer these questions.

Who

1 . . . stayed out of the room, in order to leave Oliver and Jenny alone?

2 . . . had won a scholarship to study in Paris?

3 . . . said, 'What about our marriage?'

4 . . . made polite small talk during dinner?

5 . . . was the new head of the Peace Corps?

Read Chapter 4. Are these sentences true (T) or false (F)? Change the false sentences into true ones.

1 Jenny thought that Oliver was rebelling against his father.

2 Mr Barrett was against the marriage because he thought Jenny was unsuitable.

3 Oliver said that he didn't want his father's money.

4 Phil Cavilleri wanted to telephone Oliver's father.

5 Oliver was able to get a scholarship for law school.

6 Both Jenny's and Oliver's fathers came to the wedding.

Before you read the rest of the story, can you guess what happens? Choose Y (Yes) or N (No) for each of these ideas.

1 For three years Oliver and Jenny are happy. Y/N

2 Later, they argue a lot and their marriage fails. Y/N

3 Mr Barrett pays for Oliver's studies at law school. Y/N

4 Oliver finishes law school and gets a good job. Y/N

5 Jenny tries to bring Oliver and his father together. Y/N

6 Oliver never sees or speaks to his father again. Y/N

Read Chapter 5. Choose the best question-word for each of these questions, and then answer the questions.

How / What / Who / Why

1 . . . did Jenny do all day while Oliver was at law school?
2 . . . arrived in the post one day?
3 . . . spoke to Mr Barrett on the telephone?
4 . . . was Jenny angry with Oliver?
5 . . . threw the telephone across the room?
6 . . . did Oliver feel when he saw Jenny sitting on the step?

Read Chapter 6, and then complete these sentences. (Use as many words as you like.)

1 After Oliver finished law school, he _____.
2 For the first time in three years, they _____.
3 They went to see a doctor because _____.
4 The doctor later told Oliver that _____.
5 One evening Jenny asked Oliver to _____.
6 They had never thought about _____.

Read Chapter 7, and then answer these questions.

1 Why did Oliver go to see his father?
2 He told his father a lie. What was it?
3 What did Phil do when he heard the news about Jenny?
4 What was the last thing that Jenny asked Oliver to do?
5 Why do you think that Oliver said to his father, 'Love means you never have to say you're sorry'?

After Reading

1 Complete this paragraph about Jenny, using some of the words below. Then write a paragraph about Oliver, using the words which are left. One of the words can describe both of them. Which is it?

baker / banker / beautiful / Boston / clever / close to / cold / famous / good-looking / Harvard / ice hockey / Italian / law / law school / loving / music / Paris / Phil / poor / Radcliffe / Rhode Island / rich / serious / sir / the piano / uncomfortable with / warm

Jenny is a _____, _____ young woman. She is a _____ student at _____, and she plays _____ really well. After she graduates, Jenny plans to study in _____. She comes from a _____ _____ family. Her father is a _____ from _____, and is a _____, _____ man. Jenny feels very _____ him, and calls him _____.

2 Complete this conversation between Jenny and her father. (Use as many words as you like.)

JENNY: Phil, I've met the man I'm going to marry!
PHIL: You have? Well, who is he?
JENNY: He's _____.
PHIL: And what does he do, this Oliver Barrett?
JENNY: He's _____.
PHIL: So what's he like? A music-lover like you?

JENNY: Oh no, _____.

PHIL: I see. So how long have you known him?

JENNY: Only _____.

PHIL: That's not long, Jenny. Are you sure about this?

JENNY: Yes, I am. I've never _____.

PHIL: That's OK, then. So, when's the wedding?

JENNY: As soon as _____.

PHIL: So soon? Well, when am I going to meet him?

JENNY: Can we _____?

PHIL: Of course! I'll start baking some cakes today.

Now write the conversation between Oliver and his parents, when he tells them about Jenny.

3 **When the invitation came, Oliver said to Jenny, 'Write them a nice letter of refusal'. Put the words below in the best order, join them into sentences, and write her letter.**

1 and he just couldn't get back to Harvard in time

2 which arrived this morning

3 with love from Oliver and Jenny

4 you see, he has a very important exam that morning . . .

5 thank you very much for the kind invitation . . .

6 but we hope you have a wonderful party . . .

7 dear Mr and Mrs Barrett

8 but we're afraid that we won't be able to . . .

9 and we wish Mr Barrett a very happy birthday

10 Oliver and I would love to come . . .

11 because Oliver has to be at Harvard the next day

12 we are really very sorry about this . . .

4 Perhaps Mr Barrett found out about Jenny by phoning Ray Stratton. Put their conversation in the correct order, and write in the speakers' names.

1 _____ 'Well, sir . . .'
2 _____ 'Tell me the truth. What kind of trouble is he in?'
3 _____ 'How ill, Ray?'
4 _____ 'You're welcome, sir.'
5 _____ 'I'm phoning about Oliver. I'm worried about him.'
6 _____ 'This is Oliver Barrett the Third here, calling from Boston.'
7 _____ 'I'll go there immediately. Thank you for your help.'
8 _____ 'Mr Barrett? What can I do for you, sir?'
9 _____ 'I'm so sorry to tell you this, but it's Jenny . . . she's ill.'
10 _____ 'Hello, Stratton speaking.'
11 _____ 'Very ill indeed. She's in New York City Hospital.'

5 **What do you think is important when you choose someone to marry? Add two more ideas of your own to this list, then number them all 1 to 12 (with 1 for the most important).**

A good husband or wife should . . .
- be good-looking
- be from a rich family
- be fun to be with
- have the same interests as you
- be younger or older than you

- be kind
- be intelligent
- be honest
- be loving
- be patient

6 **Look at these problems, and decide what you would do. Choose a, b, or c, and explain why.**

   1 Someone wants to go out with you. Their home, family, and interests are very different from yours. Do you . . .
   a) say no   b) say yes   c) agree to be just friends

   2 You have a scholarship to study in another country. Before you go, you meet someone and fall in love. Do you . . .
   a) go   b) stay   c) ask him or her to go with you

   3 You plan to get married very soon. Your parents say they don't want you to do this. Do you . . .
   a) obey them   b) marry now   c) plan to marry much later

   4 Your wife or husband is very ill. Your company gives you an important job to do in another town. Do you . . .
   a) accept   b) refuse   c) say you'll think about it

7 **Look at these well-known sayings about love. Do you agree or disagree with them? Why? Can you think of any more sayings which begin: 'Love is . . .' or 'Love means . . .'?**

   • Love means you never have to say you're sorry.
   • Love is blind.
   • All you need is love.
   • Love will find a way.
   • Love makes the world go round.
   • All's fair in love and war.

ABOUT THE AUTHOR

Erich Segal was born in America in 1937, and studied at Harvard University. *Love Story*, his first novel, was written in 1970. It became a world-wide bestseller, with over 21 million copies sold in 33 languages. A film of the book was made in the same year, starring Ryan O'Neal and Ali McGraw. This was also an immediate success. It had seven Oscar nominations, and won Segal a Golden Globe award for his filmscript.

Segal has written many other bestsellers, and several of them have been filmed. One of his most well-known films is the Beatles' *Yellow Submarine*. In 1977 he wrote *Oliver's Story*, which is about what happens to Oliver Barrett after Jenny's death. Segal's latest novel is called *Only Love*.

As well as these popular novels, he has written many serious works about Latin and Greek. Professor Segal now lives in England and is a Fellow of Wolfson College, Oxford.

ABOUT BOOKWORMS

OXFORD BOOKWORMS LIBRARY

*Classics • True Stories • Fantasy & Horror • Human Interest
Crime & Mystery • Thriller & Adventure*

The OXFORD BOOKWORMS LIBRARY offers a wide range of original and adapted stories, both classic and modern, which take learners from elementary to advanced level through six carefully graded language stages:

Stage 1 (400 headwords)	**Stage 4** (1400 headwords)
Stage 2 (700 headwords)	**Stage 5** (1800 headwords)
Stage 3 (1000 headwords)	**Stage 6** (2500 headwords)

More than fifty titles are also available on cassette, and there are many titles at Stages 1 to 4 which are specially recommended for younger learners. In addition to the introductions and activities in each Bookworm, resource material includes photocopiable test worksheets and Teacher's Handbooks, which contain advice on running a class library and using cassettes, and the answers for the activities in the books.

Several other series are linked to the OXFORD BOOKWORMS LIBRARY. They range from highly illustrated readers for young learners, to playscripts, non-fiction readers, and unsimplified texts for advanced learners.

Oxford Bookworms Starters	*Oxford Bookworms Factfiles*
Oxford Bookworms Playscripts	*Oxford Bookworms Collection*

Details of these series and a full list of all titles in the OXFORD BOOKWORMS LIBRARY can be found in the *Oxford English* catalogues. A selection of titles from the OXFORD BOOKWORMS LIBRARY can be found on the next pages.

Ethan Frome

EDITH WHARTON

Retold by Susan Kingsley

Life is always hard for the poor, in any place and at any time. Ethan Frome is a farmer in Massachusetts. He works long hours every day, but his farm makes very little money. His wife, Zeena, is a thin, grey woman, always complaining, and only interested in her own ill health.

Then Mattie Silver, a young cousin, comes to live with the Fromes, to help Zeena and do the housework. Her bright smile and laughing voice bring light and hope into the Fromes' house – and into Ethan's lonely life.

But poverty is a prison from which few people escape . . .

Go, Lovely Rose and Other Stories

H. E. BATES

Retold by Rosemary Border

A warm summer night. The moon shines down on the quiet houses and gardens. Everyone is asleep. Everyone except the man in pyjamas and slippers, standing on the wet grass at the end of his garden, watching and waiting . . .

In these three short stories, H. E. Bates presents ordinary people like you and me. But as we get to know them better, we see that their feelings are not at all ordinary. In fact, what happens to them – and in them – is passionate, and even extraordinary. Could this happen to you and me?

BOOKWORMS • THRILLER & ADVENTURE • STAGE 3

The Prisoner of Zenda

ANTHONY HOPE

Retold by Diane Mowat

'We must leave for Zenda at once, to find the King!' cried Sapt. 'If we're caught, we'll all be killed!'

So Rudolf Rassendyll and Sapt gallop through the night to find the King of Ruritania. But the King is now a prisoner in the Castle of Zenda. Who will rescue him from his enemies, the dangerous Duke Michael and Rupert of Hentzau?

And who will win the heart of the beautiful Princess Flavia?

BOOKWORMS • CLASSICS • STAGE 3

The Call of the Wild

JACK LONDON

Retold by Nick Bullard

When men find gold in the frozen north of Canada, they need dogs – big, strong dogs to pull the sledges on the long journeys to and from the gold mines.

Buck is stolen from his home in the south and sold as a sledge-dog. He has to learn a new way of life – how to work in harness, how to stay alive in the ice and the snow . . . and how to fight. Because when a dog falls down in a fight, he never gets up again.

Tooth and Claw

SAKI

Retold by Rosemary Border

Conradin is ten years old. He lives alone with his aunt. He has two big secrets. The first is that he hates his aunt. The second is that he keeps a small, wild animal in the garden shed. The animal has sharp, white teeth, and it loves fresh blood. Every night, Conradin prays to this animal and asks it to do one thing for him, just one thing.

This collection of short stories is clever, funny, and shows us 'Nature, red in tooth and claw'. In other words, it is Saki at his very best.

Washington Square

HENRY JAMES

Retold by Kieran McGovern

When a handsome young man begins to court Catherine Sloper, she feels she is very lucky. She is a quiet, gentle girl, but neither beautiful nor clever; no one had ever admired her before, or come to the front parlour of her home in Washington Square to whisper soft words of love to her.

But in New York in the 1840s young ladies are not free to marry where they please. Catherine must have her father's permission, and Dr Sloper is a rich man. One day Catherine will have a fortune of 30,000 dollars a year . . . ✗